NETFLIX

CUPHEAD © and ™ 2022 StudioMDHR Entertainment Inc.

THE CUPHEAD SHOW! ™ Based on the video game from StudioMDHR.

Netflix™: Netflix, Inc. Used with permission.

Published in the United States by Random House Children's Books, a division of Penguin Random House LLC, 1745 Broadway, New York, NY 10019, and in Canada by Penguin Random House Canada Limited, Toronto. Random House and the colophon are registered trademarks of Penguin Random House LLC.

RHCBOOKS.COM

Library of Congress Cataloging-in-Publication Data is available upon request.

ISBN 978-0-593-4-3202-0 (trade) — ISBN 978-0-593-4-3203-7 (ebook)

Printed in the United States of America

10 9 8 7 6 5 4 3 2 1

THE CUPHEAD SHOW!

HANDLE WITH CARE

FEATURING

"HANDLE WITH CARE"

AND

"BRINGING UP BABY BOTTLE"

RANDOM HOUSE 🏠 NEW YORK

HANDLE WITH CARE

AHHHHH!

AHHH!

BOY, THAT NEVER GETS EASIER.

DON'T WORRY JUST YET!

FWISH FWISH FWISH FWISH

HOW DO I LOOK?

GOOD AS NEW!

CLATTER!

SPLICK

AAAAND, VOILA!

THANKS, CUPHEAD!

DRIP DRIP

WELL, DON'T GET MAD AT *ME*.

WELL, DON'T GET MAD AT *ME*!

I'M THE ONE OVER HERE RACKIN' MY BRAIN TRYIN' TO REMEMBER WHAT GLUE IS!

HEY, THAT'S RIGHT!

GLUE IS GLUE!

HERE WE GO!

23

24

25

EEGGGGGHHHH...

YUP. ANYWAY, I'LL SELL YA THE GLUE. BE BACK IN A JIF.

YA SEE, MUGMAN? NOTHIN' TO WORRY ABOUT. THAT HANDLE WILL BE BACK ON IN NO TIME.

THAT IS...IF YOU EVEN *WANT* IT BACK.

MAYBE IT'S TIME FOR A LITTLE CHANGE...

LISTEN, CUPHEAD, I DON'T WANT ANY OF THESE OTHER HANDLES. I JUST WANNA BE *ME* AGAIN.

AH YES, THE OL' CLASSIC. WE'LL STICK WITH THE ORIGINAL!

RIGHT!

WRONG! I'M ALL OUTTA GLUE. I GET THE NEXT SHIPMENT IN THREE MONTHS.

THREE MONTHS?!

AW, C'MON, MUGSY! THREE MONTHS'LL GO BY LIKE *THAT!* AND HEY, YOU CAN STILL GO OUTSIDE!

PEOPLE JUST NEED TO GET USED TO IT!

REALLY?

WHHAAAAAAA!!!

SORRY, I'M STILL GETTING USED TO IT.

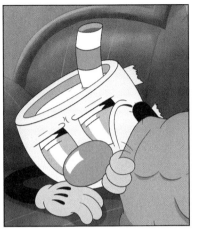

UHH, MUGMAN? OH, THERE YOU ARE, BOY!

EXCUSE US FOR A MOMENT, CUPHEAD.

OF COURSE. I'LL LEAVE YOU TWO ALONE.

I WAS IN THE MIDDLE OF BRUSHING MY TINY LITTLE TOOTHY...

...WHEN TO MY SURPRISE, IT HAPPENED!

POP!

DARN IT IF MY BABY HANDLE DIDN'T JUST POP RIGHT OFF!

COCK-A-DOODLE-DOO!

IN THE MORNING, I RAN OVER TO MY BEDROOM MIRROR...

...AND THERE IT WAS...MY SHINY NEW...MAN-HANDLE!

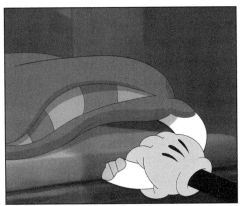

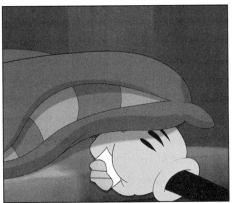

ZZZZ...

ZZZZ...

COCK-A-DOODLE-DOO!

ELDER KETTLE,
ELDER KETTLE,
ELDER KETTLE!

39

BRINGING UP
BABY BOTTLE

WELL, IT'S THAT TIME AGAIN, BOYS...

I'M OFF TO MY WEEKLY MUSTACHE WAX.

NOW, REMEMBER...

TWO RULES WHILE I'M GONE.

NUMBER ONE--DON'T TOUCH MY RADIO.

IT IS MY MOST *PRIZED* POSSESSION, AFTER ALL.

AND, OF COURSE, RULE NUMBER TWO-- *NO FIGHTING!*

SLAM

BONK
WHAM
POW

HOLD IT!

SAY, CUPHEAD, WHY'RE WE FIGHTIN' AGAIN?

UH, 'CAUSE WE'RE NOT S'POSED TO?

RIGHT!

MAYBE HE NEEDS HIS DIAPER CHANGED?

OR I COULD TRY BURPING HIM AGAIN.

YEAH, TRY THAT SOME MORE. THAT'S A GREAT IDEA.

IT'S ALL RIGHT, BABY.

WAHHH!

BURP!

THERE...THAT'S BETTER.

MAMA!

RRIIPPP

BABY!!!

WHAM

HEE-HEE!

EASY...

EASY...

OHHH, COME ON!

CUPHEAD! GLASS ON THE FLOOR?! BABY COULD GET HURT!

WELL, *BABY* BROKE THE FISHBOWL!

OPEN THE DOOR! BABY!

MUGMAN, YA GOTTA LISTEN TO ME. THERE'S SOMETHING WRONG WITH THAT BABY! WE GOTTA GET RID OF IT!

NOT A CHANCE, CUPHEAD! BABY NEEDS OUR LOVE!

WHAT IT NEEDS IS A LEASH!

CUPHEAD, THE WAY YOU'RE TALKIN', IT'S LIKE YOU NEVER EVEN WANTED A BABY!

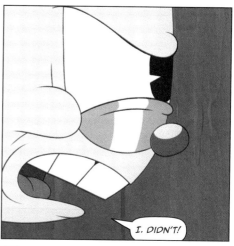

I. DIDN'T!

≶GASP≷ OH WELL, THEN I GUESS I'LL DO ALL THE PARENTING MYSELF.

BE MY GUEST!

HMPH!

KNOCK KNOCK KNOCK

64

NO! BAD BABY! BAD!

MAMA...

UH, I DON'T LIKE THAT CRAZY GLINT IN HIS EYE.

OH, NONSENSE, CUPHEAD.

BUT--

CALM. DOWN. WAIT RIGHT THERE.

I'VE HAD THIS BEAR SINCE I WAS A TINY BABY.

IT MEANS THE WORLD TO ME.

CRANK
CRANK

IT WAS ALWAYS THERE TO CHEER ME UP. AND NOW IT'LL BE THERE FOR *YOU*.

HAHA.

RRIIPPP

AHHHHH!

I'M GONNA KILL THAT THING!

MUGMAN, NO! IT'S A BABY!

IT'S NOT A BABY! IT'S EVIL!

≥GASP≤

IT'S GONE!

71

THE END

NETFLIX

THE CUPHEAD SHOW!

EXECUTIVE PRODUCER – DAVE WASSON

EXECUTIVE PRODUCER – CJ KETTLER

EXECUTIVE PRODUCER – CHAD MOLDENHAUER

EXECUTIVE PRODUCER – JARED MOLDENHAUER

CO-EXECUTIVE PRODUCER – COSMO SEGURSON

BASED ON THE VIDEO GAME BY STUDIO MDHR

DEVELOPED BY DAVE WASSON

SUPERVISING DIRECTOR – CLAY MORROW

SUPERVISING DIRECTOR – ADAM PALOIAN

WRITTEN BY – DEEKI DEKE

ART DIRECTOR – ANDREA FERNANDEZ

BOOK DESIGN – NEIL ERICKSON